Snowshoe Hare

Black Bear

River
Otter

THE *Spirit Trackers*

FIFTH
HOUSE

BY JAN BOURDEAU WABOOSE
ILLUSTRATED BY FRANÇOIS THISDALE

ACKNOWLEDGEMENTS

Special thanks to Kathryn Cole, the most perceptive editor
of Indigenous values I have worked with.

Also much thanks to François Thisdale for his appreciation,
and vivid, detailed imaginings of native storytelling.

Working with both of them was my pleasure.

—JBW

Copyright ©2018 Jan Bourdeau Waboose

Illustrations ©2018 François Thisdale

Published in the United States in 2018.

Published in Canada by Fifth House Publishers
195 Allstate Parkway, Markham, ON L3R 4T8

Published in the United States by Fifth House Publishers
311 Washington Street, Brighton, MA 02135

10 9 8 7 6 5 4 3 2 1

Fifth House Publishers acknowledges with thanks the Canada Council for the Arts and the
Ontario Arts Council for their support of our publishing program.

Waboose, Jan Bourdeau, author
The spirit trackers / by Jan Bourdeau Waboose ; illustrated
by François Thisdale.
ISBN 978-1-927083-11-6 (hardcover)
I. Thisdale, François, 1964-, illustrator II. Title.
PS8595.A26S65 2017   jC813'.54   C2017-905328-0

Publisher Cataloging-in-Publication Data (U.S.)
Names: Waboose, Jan Bourdeau, author. | Thisdale, François, 1964-, illustrator.
Title: Spirit Trackers / by Jan Bourdeau Waboose ; illustrated by François Thisdale.
Description: Markham, Ontario : Fifth House Publishers, 2017. | Summary: "Native telling of the Windigo,
the Night Spirit of Winter, told by an uncle elder to two Aboriginal cousins, and the tracking of the feared
creature into the forest. This illustrated book is a heartwarming story of family, love, togetherness
and respect for the environment" – Provided by publisher.
Identifiers: ISBN 978-1-92708-311-6 (hardcover)

Subjects: LCSH: Windigos – Juvenile fiction. | Indians of North America – Folklore |
BISAC: JUVENILE FICTION / Fairy Tales & Folklore / General.
Classification: LCC E98.F6W336 | DDC 398.208997 – dc23

Designed by Tanya Montini

Printed in Hong Kong by Sheck Wah Tong

*I want to thank the Windigo Spirits for sharing
the story of our peoples' ways. I offer tobacco
and acknowledge them. Meegwetch.*

*For Uncle Basil, and all of his nephews and nieces,
who think he is the Best Uncle ever. BBB*

*To the memory of my grandfather, Lucien,
and the magical time he spent feeding my dreams
with word paintings.*
—F.T.

"These are Makwasaagim—Trackers' shoes," says Uncle. "Trackers are in our family."

"That's what I am," says Tom, "a Tracker."

"Me too," Cousin Will nods as Uncle hangs the snowshoes on the shed wall.

"Our grandfathers walked many trails in their snowshoes during the time of the Freezing Spirit Moon. Their moosehide clothing protected them from the bitter cold. The moose has given much to our people, and that is why we honour the great animal. That is why our family is the Moose Clan."

Uncle's eyes glisten like pebbles in a cold stream as he touches the beaded moose on his winter jacket.

Tom and Will touch the moose on their jackets.

Together, they speak in a whisper.

"Uncle, tell us the story of the *Windigo*."

The boys look behind them for something they can't see.

Uncle sits on a frozen birch log. Tom and Will sit on the snow quilt. The wind whines and wails above their heads, shaking the cedars. A pair of ravens perch on the clothesline, waiting for the story to begin.

"The W-i-n-d-i-g-o, the Wandering Night Spirit of Winter, is out there."

Uncle raises his arms to the darkening sky.

"The Windigo is to be feared. It howls loud enough to bring fierce blizzards with snow deep enough to bury you. It clouds your eyes and numbs your nose until you cannot breathe. The Windigo will make you lose your way.

Uncle's frosty breath hangs in the air, forming ghostly white images.

His voice grows louder.

"Watch out for the Windigo on a winter night. It has a heart of ice, and its teeth are like steel. It will eat anything in its way!"

Suddenly, the ravens scream, and are gone. Will looks to the house. Tom does too. Uncle continues.

"Even the best Trackers disappear in Windigo's footsteps.

Never look into its eyes." Uncle jumps up, throws his head back like a huge bear, and roars with laughter.

"You can't run from the Windigo!"

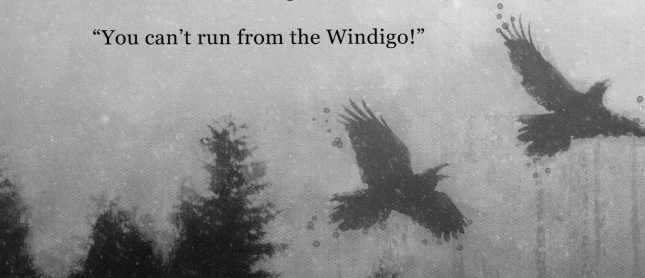

As they head to the house, Uncle wraps his strong arms around them.

"Remember," he says, "winter can be dangerous to all things. Respect it and always honour the animals who face the Windigo."

That night, Will and Tom lie under moosehide covers, but sleep does not come to them.

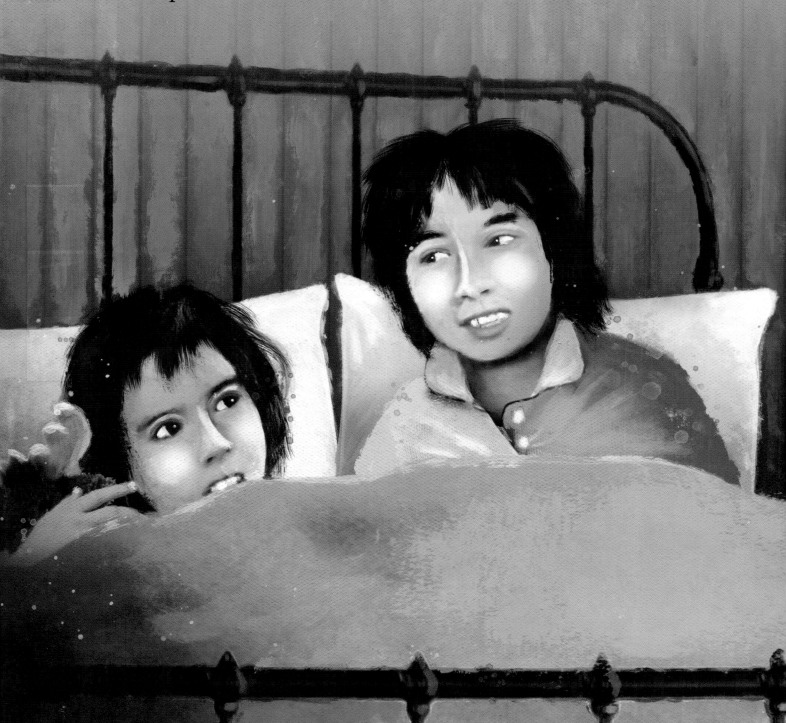

"You still going to be a Tracker?" asks Will.

"Said I was, and I will," replies Tom. "I'm not scared of the Windigo." His face does not match his brave words. "What about you?"

"I'm a Tracker too," answers Will. "But let's sleep now. No more talking." *At least not about the Windigo,* he thinks.

"Wake up!" Tom's voice rattles the night. "Do you hear that?"

Will listens in the dark. "Can't hear anything," he says.
"Probably just a dream."

"No. I heard it by the window," says Tom.

Will is afraid to know what the sound is. "Go to sleep,"
he says.

"Fine," says Tom. He doesn't want to know, either.

Just as sleep returns, *Thump! Bang!* A huge black shadow crosses the window. With eyes wide, the cousins stare at each other.

"Good Trackers would go and look," Tom whispers.

"Let's go," says Will. "You coming?"

Both boys slink to the window like night hunters. They try to peer out, but there is frost on the glass. Then comes a frightening sound, and the black shadow presses against the pane.

"The Windigo!" The boys run to their bed and burrow under the comfort of their covers.

"How did you two sleep?" asks Uncle in the morning.

"Soundly," says Tom, looking at his feet.

"Soundly," says Will, poking at his breakfast bannock.

They don't tell Uncle they were scared of the night, but go outside, and run to the bedroom window.

"Look! Huge, deep tracks!" Tom points to the footprints leading from the window to the birch trees.

"Whoa, look at that tree. Something's ripped the bark clear off!" shouts Will. Both boys notice large tracks going across the field and into the pines.

"What do you think it is?" asks Tom.

Will shrugs. "What do you think?"

Tom shrugs back.

The cousins stand like totems. Each knows what the other is thinking.

Both know what they must do.

In the shed, Tom and Will strap on their Makwasaagims.

"Who wants to track first?" asks Tom.

"It's okay if you do," says Will.

"Chi-meegwetch—thanks—but it's okay if you do."

"You sure?" asks Will, hoping Tom will change his mind. Tom doesn't.

The winter wind howls and whips snow in their faces as they go. It stings their eyes and bites their skin, leaving their cheeks red. Wind and snow cover the tracks, making them impossible to follow. Uncle's house is nowhere in sight.

"Let's take cover under that big Jack pine.

Your legs must be tired," says Tom.

"Not mine," says Will. "Yours must be."

"It's warmer here," says Tom, "but we've come a long way
and we should get home. Whatever made those tracks is
gone. I know. I'm a good Tracker."

"Right. I'm a good Tracker too," boasts Will.

Tom removes his mitts to wipe his nose, but Will's sudden
scream stops him. The branch above their heads is stripped
of its needles! Eaten clean away. The boys' eyes are as large
as the Freezing Spirit Moon.

Wandering night spirit...it eats anything in its path!

A dark shadow skitters past and is gone.

"The Windigo!" screams Will.

"It was only a lynx," whispers Tom. But the reassuring words
are for himself.

"Let's get outta here!" they say together.

No sooner are the words spoken, than a sad cry slices the air like a trapper's knife. The sound—not human—echoes in their ears. Neither boy can move. The snowshoes that carried them this far are now keeping them from running.

Another long, haunting cry and another, over and over.

"It's hungry," mutters Will. He thinks of frozen, steel teeth.

The cries grow weak...almost pleading.

The boys are terrified, but they know what good Trackers must do. They edge closer to the sound.

"Remember," Will whispers, "don't look into its eyes."

In front of them, a huge dark shape lies in the snow.

It raises its enormous head and bellows.

Its charcoal eyes pierce them.

It struggles to stand up.

You can't run from the Windigo!

Hot air huffs from the huge nose.

"Wait," shouts Tom. "It's not a—"

"It's a moose!"

The young animal struggles again to get up, but his long legs are buried in snow. His cry is a whimper now. Tom and Will approach carefully.

Honour the animals who face the Windigo.

Will and Tom dig frantically. The moose lies still and cold. Tom reaches over and with a gentle touch, rubs the velvet nose. Will does too.

The moose breathes softer and does not move. Then, with quick thrusts, his legs are free. He shakes himself and stands tall. The boys look into his eyes. He nods his large head twice and disappears into the night.

"There you are!" calls Uncle. "It's time for good Trackers to come home."

"Yeah," say Tom and Will together. Their eyes glisten like pebbles in a cold stream as they touch the beaded moose on their jackets. "And we have a Windigo story to tell you."

Uncle smiles and wraps his strong arms around them. And the three Trackers head home under the Freezing Spirit Moon.

The Windigo is known in the minds and lives of Anishinaabe peoples, as it is essential for survival in the north country winters. There are many stories of the Windigo from Native tribes. The Windigo is feared and respected by Anishinaabe peoples. It is said that the Windigo can transform itself into human or animal shape and can walk on the wind in the icy northern wilderness. Its giant spirit will hunt for Native people who are lost in the frozen winter bush! Strange unexplained sights and sounds come from the dark forest at night. It is the Windigo.

Many stories are told to keep children away from the dangers of winter blizzards and to stop them from wandering away. Protection from Windigo is the strength and love of family. This love is powerful enough to scare the Windigo away and keep you safe.

But don't talk of Windigo before the ice forms...or else....

Northern Cardinal

Wolf

Moose